This book belongs to

_____

Written by Katherine Sully
Illustrated by Janet Samuel
Designed by Chris Fraser at
Page to Page

This edition published by Parragon Books Ltd in 2014

Parragon Books Ltd
Chartist House
15–17 Trim Street
Bath BA1 1HA, UK
www.parragon.com

ISBN 978-1-4723-7722-7

Printed in China

Where, Oh Where Is Huggle Buggle Bear?

PaRRagon

Bath • New York • Cologne • Melbourne • Delhi
Hong Kong • Shenzhen • Singapore • Amsterdam

Where, oh where is **Huggle Buggle** Bear?
I can't find him anywhere!
He always hides when it's time for bed.
He is such a **funny** bear!

Is he snacking on toast and honey,
Making crumbs with **Babbity Bunny**?

No!
He isn't with
Babbity Bunny.

It's way past **Huggle Buggle**'s bedtime
And I'm feeling very cross.
I can't go to bed without him.
I hope he isn't lost!

Where, oh where is **Huggle Buggle** Bear?
I can't find him anywhere!
He always hides when it's time for bed.
He is such a **silly** bear!

Is he bouncing on his belly,
On the sofa with Ellie Nellie?

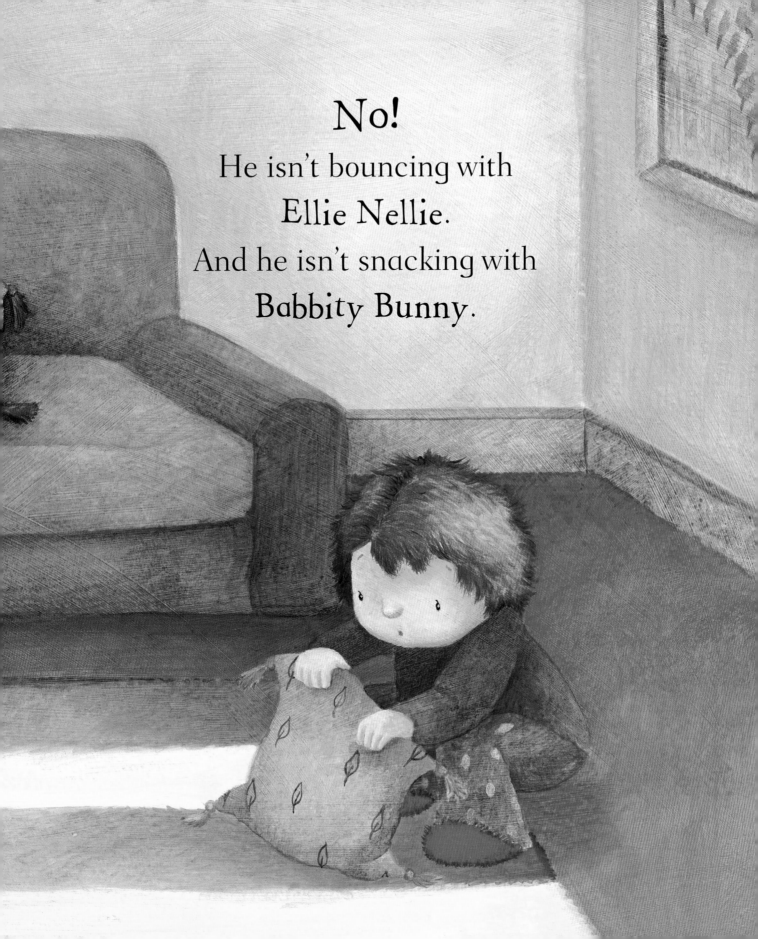

No!
He isn't bouncing with
Ellie Nellie.
And he isn't snacking with
Babbity Bunny.

It's way past **Huggle Buggle**'s bedtime
And I'm feeling very sleepy.
I can't go to bed without him,
It's much too dark and creepy.

Where, oh where is **Huggle Buggle** Bear?
I can't find him anywhere!
He always hides when it's time for bed.
He is such a **naughty** bear!

Is he making lots of noise
With Woolly Lamb and the other toys?

No!

He isn't playing with
Woolly Lamb.
He isn't bouncing with
Ellie Nellie.
He isn't snacking with
Babbity Bunny.

It's way past **Huggle Buggle**'s bedtime
And now I'm feeling worried.
I can't go to bed without him.
That would be really horrid.

Where, oh where is **Huggle Buggle** Bear?
I can't find him anywhere!
He always hides when it's time for bed.
He is such a **bothersome** bear.

Is he splashing in the tub,
Blowing bubbles with **Rubadub**?

No!
He isn't splashing with
Rubadub.
He isn't playing with
Woolly Lamb.
He isn't bouncing with
Ellie Nellie.
He isn't snacking with
Babbity Bunny.

It's way past **Huggle Buggle**'s bedtime
And now I'm feeling sad.
I don't want to go to bed without him,
But I think I'd better had...

I know where...
there's Huggle Buggle Bear!
And all the other toys.
I think they must be fast asleep,
So, **sssh!** Don't make a noise!

The End